Mrs. Jeepers in Outer Space

by Debbie Dadey
and
Marcia Thornton Jones

illustrated by John Steven Gurney

A
LITTLE APPLE
PAPERBACK

SCHOLASTIC INC.
New York   Toronto   London   Auckland   Sydney
Mexico City   New Delhi   Hong Kong

*To all the scientists and astronauts who help make
dreams a reality. — MTJ*

For my new son, Alex Dadey, with love — DD

*And to the fantastic members of the Mercury Team:
Nathan Dadey, my fantastic son; Katie Lavery Niekamp,
our most excellent leader; Ron, Debby, Geoffry, and
Stephan Cantley; Haley and Stuart Doloboff, Brian and
David Carstens, Corey and Jeff Cox.*

No part of this publication may be reproduced in whole or in part, or stored
in a retrieval system, or transmitted in any form or by any means,
electronic, mechanical, photocopying, recording, or otherwise, without
written permission of the publisher. For information regarding permission,
write to Scholastic Inc., Attention: Permissions Department, 555 Broadway,
New York, NY 10012.

ISBN 0-439-04396-4

Text copyright © 1999 by Marcia Thornton Jones and Debra S. Dadey.
Illustrations copyright © 1999 by Scholastic Inc.
All rights reserved. Published by Scholastic Inc.
SCHOLASTIC, LITTLE APPLE PAPERBACKS, THE ADVENTURES OF THE BAILEY
SCHOOL KIDS, and associated logos are trademarks and/or registered
trademarks of Scholastic Inc.

12 11 10 9 8 7 6 5 4   9/9 0 1 2 3 4/0

Printed in the U.S.A.   40

First Scholastic printing, July 1999

Contents

1

BLAST

"What are you doing?" Melody asked her friend Howie. It was before school on Monday and Melody, Howie, and Liza were in their favorite meeting place.

Howie danced around the oak tree and sang, "This is so cool! This is fantastic!"

"What's so fantastic?" Liza dropped her blue Bailey School backpack under the oak tree and stared at Howie. Usually Howie was calm. Not today.

Howie stopped dancing for a second. "I can't say until Eddie gets here."

"School is a waste of time," Eddie said, walking up beside Liza. "Why would I want to be early for school?"

"Because," Howie said with a big smile, "I have the greatest news ever."

"Mrs. Jeepers is moving away?" Eddie said hopefully. Their third-grade teacher, Mrs. Jeepers, was unlike any teacher they'd ever seen. Some of the kids in their class even thought Mrs. Jeepers was a vampire.

Howie shook his head. "This is even better. We're going on a field trip next Monday!"

Melody, Liza, and Eddie all groaned together. "What's so great about that?" Melody asked. "Mrs. Jeepers never lets us go anyplace fun."

"She will this time," Howie said. "My dad made all the arrangements." Howie's dad worked at F.A.T.S., the Federal Aeronautics Technology Station, on the outskirts of town.

Liza stomped her foot. "Will you please tell us where we're going?"

"Space," Howie said. "Well, a camp about space, to be exact. F.A.T.S. is sponsoring a weeklong camp for the third grade. It's called the Bailey Lunar Astronaut Student Training Camp. BLAST Camp for short. It's going to have equipment and stuff like the real astronauts use."

Eddie grabbed the baseball cap off his red hair and threw it up in the air. Liza giggled and Melody did a cartwheel. Howie danced around the oak tree one more time.

"Does this mean we get to miss school for a whole week?" Eddie asked.

Howie nodded. "It sure does. And if we're lucky we might even get to meet a real astronaut."

"Holy Toledo!" Eddie yelled. "This is too good to be true!"

"Maybe it is," Liza said softly. "Will Mrs. Jeepers be going with us to camp?"

Howie sat down with his back to the trunk of the oak tree. "I suppose so."

Liza pushed a strand of blond hair out of her face. "Then I don't know if BLAST Camp is such a good idea."

"Are you crazy?" Eddie asked. "This is

the best part of third grade. It's about time something good happened. I'm tired of science tests and social studies reports."

Liza pointed her finger at Eddie. "First of all, it sounds a little dangerous. And second of all, I don't like the idea of spending a whole week with Mrs. Jeepers at a camp."

Melody gulped. "Liza's right. There's no telling what a vampire teacher could do to a bunch of kids at a camp away from home."

"I could tell you some things," Eddie said, "but I don't think you want to hear them."

The bell rang to start school and the kids headed toward the building. "Don't worry," Howie told them. "There will be plenty of scientists like my dad around to protect us from bloodsucking teachers."

"Who's going to protect the scientists?" Melody asked.

Eddie grinned. "I guess that's up to us."

2

Space Shuttle

"I don't want to ride this stupid bus," Eddie complained on the way to the brand-new BLAST Camp. "I want to drive a space shuttle." Eddie pretended to drive a spaceship, complete with roaring sounds. "Zoom. Zoom!" he roared, turning a pretend steering wheel.

"You're driving me insane," Melody said from the seat in front of Eddie. "Why don't you be quiet?"

Eddie stuck his tongue out at Melody, but Howie put his hand on Eddie's shoulder. "I'm pretty sure there's no noise in space," Howie told him.

Mrs. Jeepers turned around in her seat at the front of the bus. "Space is silent," Mrs. Jeepers said in her strange accent.

"As this bus should be. Let me tell you more facts about space."

Eddie groaned, but he stopped when Mrs. Jeepers flashed her green eyes at him and put her hand on the brooch she always wore. Most kids in third grade believed Mrs. Jeepers' glowing green pin was magic. All she had to do was touch it and her students knew they'd better behave.

"There are nine planets in our solar system," Mrs. Jeepers told them.

Howie raised his hand. "My dad said some scientists think Pluto is only an asteroid," he said. "That means there are only eight planets."

"That we know about," Mrs. Jeepers added. "Scientists learn more and more every day. But most people still think Pluto is a planet. All our planets revolve around the sun. Earth is the third planet from the sun. Does anyone know the fourth planet from the sun?"

Howie quickly raised his hand again and Mrs. Jeepers nodded in his direction. "It's Mars," he said proudly.

A girl named Carey raised her hand. "Mrs. Jeepers," she said, "do you think there are really Martians and other aliens?"

Mrs. Jeepers didn't answer right away. Instead, she peered out the window at the sky. Finally, she turned back to her students. "Some people believe aliens are closer than we think. Perhaps they are correct."

Mrs. Jeepers continued telling all the kids on the bus about space, but Liza whispered softly to Melody, "I wonder how Mrs. Jeepers knows so much about space."

Eddie leaned over Liza's seat to whisper. "It's because she's part alien. She probably has a spaceship in her garage."

"Shhh," Howie hissed. "I want to hear about our solar system."

Eddie rolled his eyes and got quiet, but he shouted when they pulled up in front of BLAST Camp. "Look at that!" He jumped out of his seat to get a better look at the huge space shuttle and rockets on exhibit.

Mrs. Jeepers smiled her odd little half smile. "I'm glad to see you are excited to be here, but we must remain calm."

"I can't wait," Eddie said. "I want to drive one of those babies into outer space!"

"You can't," Howie said. "Flying the space shuttle takes years of training and practice."

"I don't want to wait years and years," Eddie said, "and I definitely don't want to practice. I'm ready to lift off today and leave the rest of you in my dust — my moon dust!"

"You wouldn't leave us behind, would you?" Liza asked.

"In a nanosecond," Eddie told her.

Mrs. Jeepers stared at a life-size model

of a *Saturn V* rocket and quietly rubbed her brooch. "Liza is right. You must all stay close together this week. After all, I do not want anyone getting lost in space!"

3

Scary Alien

"'Male Habitat,'" Howie read off the side of a round metal building. "That sounds like a place for wild animals."

Melody giggled. "You and Eddie should fit in perfectly. That's where the boys stay."

While the boys stashed their gear in lockers in the Male Habitat, Liza and Melody quickly put away their backpacks in the Female Habitat and headed to the Waste Elimination Station, otherwise known as the bathroom.

"Welcome to BLAST!" A young lady in tan shorts and a blue shirt greeted the Bailey School kids and Mrs. Jeepers as they came back out of their habitats. "My name is Katy. I'll be your trainer here at BLAST Camp. Your team will be the Pluto Team."

13

Eddie leaned over to Howie. "That sounds like a dog to me."

"Great," Melody said, but she didn't sound happy. "Our team is named after a planet that some people think is just a giant rock floating in space."

"Just like the rocks in your head," Eddie said with a laugh.

Katy motioned for the kids. "Follow me to begin your space adventure!" Katy led the third-graders down a dimly lit hallway. The walls were made of cold steel and it was oddly silent. The only noise was the swishing of doors that opened automatically when they approached. The doors swished tightly closed behind them. They walked past a big door marked MUSEUM and another labeled ADVENTURE IN VENUS. Every once in a while Liza thought she heard other footsteps, but she didn't see another human being.

"Does anybody besides Katy work at BLAST Camp?" Liza whispered to Howie.

Howie nodded. "My dad said there was

an entire staff of scientists to help out. He'll even check on us from time to time."

"I wonder where they're all hiding?" Melody said as Katy led them down another corridor and into a huge room that reminded Melody of an underground cave. The walls were made of gray metal, and there wasn't a window to be seen.

"I bet Mrs. Jeepers feels right at home here," Eddie whispered. "She's safe from even a single beam of sunshine!"

Melody looked at their teacher and gulped. Mrs. Jeepers was no longer smiling her odd little half smile. Instead, she was grinning so wide Melody could see her teacher's pointy eyeteeth. Melody watched as Mrs. Jeepers reached out and gently touched the smooth walls.

The room was filled with life-size models of spaceships. Other groups of kids wandered around the room, and Melody was glad that several scientists wearing

bleached white jumpsuits were waiting for them.

"When do we get to fly a spaceship?" Eddie hollered without bothering to raise his hand.

Mrs. Jeepers flashed her green eyes in his direction. "Remember, an astronaut must study for years before getting the chance to fly into space," she told Eddie.

"That's what teachers say about everything," Eddie mumbled. "All they can think about is studying and practicing."

Katy didn't hear Eddie. "This week you will train just like real astronauts. Everyone will complete a shuttle mission here at BLAST Camp. Each of you will be either in Mission Control or on board our shuttles."

"I want to be on a shuttle!" Eddie yelled. "That's where all the important jobs are."

"Don't be so sure," Katy said. "The hard work starts right here on Earth. The shuttle crew and Mission Control crew

17

must work together. The success of every mission depends on it. Each job is important in the space program."

"That was before I got here," Eddie said, puffing out his chest. "I bet I can fly one of these babies all by myself."

Katy shook her head. "You'll need to learn a few things first," she told him.

Eddie was ready to argue, but Katy kept talking. "If you'd like, we can start by letting each of you try on a space suit."

"Cool!" Howie yelled.

Katy and the other scientists divided the kids into groups and helped them slip into kid-size space suits.

"Let me go first. I want to be the pilot," Eddie said, squeezing his way past the other kids in his group to get beside Katy. "That way I can zoom to the farthest corner of the galaxy and find scary aliens with six legs and twelve eyes."

Melody giggled. "All Eddie has to do to see a scary alien is look in the mirror."

Mrs. Jeepers shook her head. "Eddie looks nothing like an alien," she said before walking to another group of kids.

"Did you hear that?" Liza asked. "How would our teacher know what an alien looks like?"

"Easy," Eddie said. "She probably invites aliens over for Sunday dinner. Who else would want to eat her bloody recipes?"

"Shhh," Howie warned. "I can't hear what Katy is telling us."

Katy looked straight at Eddie. "Astronauts must learn all the jobs so they can pitch in and help. The success of every flight depends on that."

Each of the kids took a turn trying on a space suit. Eddie grunted when Katy put the heavy helmet on his head. He patted the thick shoulders of the suit. "I feel like a linebacker for the Green Bay Packers," he said with a laugh.

"You look just like an astronaut," Liza said.

Eddie looked at Liza in her space suit and laughed. "I always thought you were a space cadet. Now I know you are."

After trying on space suits, the kids looked at the strange equipment in the training building, but Liza grabbed Melody's arm and whispered, "Look at Mrs. Jeepers. She's so interested in space stuff, she's not paying any attention to us."

Mrs. Jeepers stood in front of a large control panel filled with buttons and knobs. She seemed fascinated by it.

"Oh, no!" Melody whimpered. "We have to do something fast, before Eddie realizes Mrs. Jeepers isn't watching us!"

But Melody was too late.

4

Space Silly

Mrs. Jeepers was the strictest teacher in the history of Bailey City. She didn't let kids get away with any mischief. When Eddie noticed his teacher was busy with the control panel, he knew it was his chance to have a little fun — space fun.

A third-grader named Huey stepped in Eddie's way. "Danger, danger," Eddie said in a robot voice. "Engage forward thrust." Eddie reached over and gave Huey a push. Huey bumped into the kids of the Saturn Team that were looking at a display of moon rocks.

Liza and Howie gasped. Melody gulped. Eddie grinned. They all looked at their teacher. Usually, Mrs. Jeepers would have her fingers on her brooch

and Eddie would have to behave. Not this time. Mrs. Jeepers was too busy studying a star map to notice.

"I don't know what to worry about most," Melody said. "The fact that Mrs. Jeepers acts like she's in outer space, or that Eddie is space silly."

Liza nodded. "Mrs. Jeepers can't look at that map forever. We have to save Eddie before it's too late."

"I think we're already too late," Melody said, pointing across the huge room. Eddie was making his way to another panel filled with buttons and switches.

Melody imagined Mission Control specialists sitting at the panel, punching buttons and twirling knobs that helped guide astronauts. But Eddie wasn't thinking about Mission Control specialists. He was too determined to be an out-of-control specialist. Before Liza and Melody could stop him, Eddie started punching buttons as if he were Beethoven playing a piano.

Liza reached Eddie first. She grabbed his arm and pulled him away from the panel. "Are you trying to blast us into space?" Liza hissed.

Eddie pulled away from Liza. "These buttons are all fakes," he said. "This whole camp is nothing but pretend. It doesn't matter what I do, so I might as well have fun."

"That's not true," Howie said, coming up to his friends. "My dad said a lot of this equipment is the real thing. We'd better pay attention. You never know when you might learn something important."

"The only things I plan to learn," Eddie said, "are new ways to have fun, fun, FUN!"

"Shhh," Melody warned, "before Mrs. Jeepers hears you."

The four friends glanced at their teacher. She was using one of her long green-painted fingernails to trace a path along the star map. "Mrs. Jeepers is too

busy making trails through the universe to notice me," Eddie said.

"That's odd," Howie said. "Why would she need to be making a space trail?"

"She shouldn't be touching that map," Liza said. "She might tear it with her long fingernails."

"Mrs. Jeepers can do whatever she wants," Eddie said, "and so can I!"

Eddie didn't wait to argue with his friends anymore. He spotted Carey skipping across the room. Eddie became an orbiting alien spaceship. He beeped. He buzzed. Eddie sputtered his way across the room until he reached Carey.

"Get out of my way," she told Eddie.

Eddie moved, but he didn't get out of the way. Instead, Eddie held out his arms and zoomed around Carey. No matter which way she turned, there he was.

"I come in peace," Eddie said in his best alien voice. "Take me to your leader."

Carey rolled her eyes. "You are worse than an alien with twelve tentacles and thirteen eyeballs," she told him. Then Carey pushed past Eddie and hurried to join a group of kids listening to Katy.

Eddie did not like being pushed. Especially by Carey. He raced across the room and sneaked up behind her.

Katy was demonstrating how astronauts use a robot arm to grab things outside their spaceship. "It is much harder than it looks," Katy was saying. "Astronauts must practice grasping things, over and over again."

Eddie made pinchers out of his fingers and thumbs and started walking like a robot. His arms, stretched straight out in front of him, looked like giant crab claws as he reached for Carey's curls.

"Don't do it," Liza whispered. But Eddie didn't listen.

"Yee-OWWW!" Carey screeched when Eddie pinched a clawful of hair and tugged.

All the kids looked at Eddie. Katy looked at Eddie, too. Then, everybody froze as Mrs. Jeepers slowly turned away from the map and flashed her green eyes in Eddie's direction.

Melody whimpered. Liza closed her eyes. Howie looked like he was about to faint. Even Eddie looked worried as Mrs. Jeepers moved toward the group of kids.

"This is the end of Eddie," Melody whispered.

5

Weightless

"He was a good friend," Liza said as she watched Mrs. Jeepers glare at Eddie.

"We'll miss him," Howie added.

But before Mrs. Jeepers could reach Eddie, Katy made her way through the group of kids and placed a hand on Eddie's shoulder. "This trainee," she said loudly enough for all to hear, "has just demonstrated how easy it is to grasp something as fine as hair. Now, let's see how well he does with the robot arm!"

Mrs. Jeepers stopped in the middle of the room and smiled her odd little half smile as Eddie was led to the mechanical arm.

"Whew," Howie said. "That was a close call."

Eddie puffed up his chest and looked

at all the kids staring at him. "This will be as easy as chewing bubble gum," he bragged. Then he grabbed the controls. The mechanical arm swung wild. Eddie jerked the controls, trying to make the arm reach down and grab a little rock. Instead, it swung straight toward Eddie's nose. Eddie yelped and jumped back.

"If that's easier than chewing gum," a boy named Jake hollered from the back of the crowd, "then don't give Eddie any bubble gum. He'd be dangerous!" The rest of the kids laughed.

Katy smiled and patted Eddie's shoulder. "Trainee Eddie has proven another valuable lesson," she said. "A mistake like this could mean life or death in outer space. Astronauts practice so mistakes can be avoided. They also practice in case mistakes happen. And all of their work is done in an environment without gravity!"

"How can they practice being weightless?" Howie asked.

Katy smiled. "I'll show you!"

Katy moved across the room, and the rest of the kids hurried after her.

"Look," Howie said, pulling his friends away from the crowd. "Mrs. Jeepers isn't interested in the star map anymore."

It was true. Mrs. Jeepers glided across the room and stared at the mechanical arm. Then their teacher grabbed the controls. It only took her one try to grasp a tiny pebble and move it to another spot.

Eddie's eyes got big. "She's good at that," he said.

"How would our teacher know how to work a robot arm?" Howie asked slowly. "Katy just said it takes lots of practice."

"BLAST Camp is new," Liza said. "Where else could Mrs. Jeepers have learned how to do that?"

"We don't have time to worry about Mrs. Jeepers," Melody said. "Katy is leaving without us."

Liza, Melody, and Eddie hurried to

catch up. Howie took one last look at his teacher before following his friends.

Katy led them into a huge room filled with gigantic metal equipment. A lot of the machines had belts and buckles. "Here is where astronauts get used to what it would be like to work without gravity," Katy told the group.

"That means they're weightless," Howie whispered.

"My mother is always on a diet," Melody said. "She'd like being weightless."

Katy pointed to another contraption that looked like a circle inside a circle inside a circle. In the very middle was a chair. "In space, there is no up or down or sideways. This machine is called a Multi-Axis Trainer. It helps space travelers get used to pitching and rolling and yawing."

"Yaw, yaw, yaw," Eddie blurted. "Let's quit this yapping and have some fun.

That thing looks like a carnival ride to me."

A quiet voice, barely louder than a whisper, stopped all the kids' giggles. Mrs. Jeepers had followed them and now she was making her way straight toward Eddie.

"It may look like fun," Mrs. Jeepers said in her Transylvanian accent. "It may even be like a carnival ride. But remember this: Everything astronauts do is serious. Deadly serious."

Eddie gulped as Mrs. Jeepers gently rubbed her green brooch. "You must pay attention to our trainer," Mrs. Jeepers told him. "Katy has much to teach us, and we are here to learn."

Katy nodded before continuing to teach the group about working in space.

"Gee," Eddie griped when he was sure Mrs. Jeepers had forgotten all about him. "Mrs. Jeepers acts like she's training to be a real astronaut."

Melody giggled. "I've never heard of a vampire astronaut before."

Howie didn't say a word. He was too busy watching his teacher.

Liza didn't talk, either. But when Katy grabbed her shoulder Liza screamed.

6

Vampernaut

"I'm not getting on that thing," Liza squealed.

"Don't be a party pooper," Eddie told her. "It'll be fun."

"Reading a book is fun," Liza said. "Riding a bike is fun, but twirling in every direction like an out-of-control airplane is not fun."

Katy smiled. "Actually, it isn't as scary as you think. And it will give you an idea of what real astronauts go through."

Liza smiled back at Katy. "Well," Liza said slowly. "If you think it's okay."

Katy strapped Liza into the Multi-Axis Trainer. Liza gulped and closed her eyes when Katy started spinning the machine.

Liza opened her eyes and giggled as

she flipped upside down. "Hey," she shouted. "This is kind of fun!"

"Let me have a turn!" Eddie yelled.

One by one, all the kids had a chance. Katy twirled them until they didn't know what was up and what was down. Katy was looking a little tired after spinning the kids, but she even gave Mrs. Jeepers a turn. Howie was the last one to go.

"Are you okay?" Melody asked Howie after he got off the machine. "You look sick."

"Do you need to go to the bathroom?" Liza asked.

"Maybe his brain is still spinning," Eddie said with a grin as Katy led them all down a long corridor. Mrs. Jeepers walked right beside a very tired-looking Katy.

Howie lagged to the back of the group so he could talk to his friends without being heard. Howie shook his head. "It's none of that."

"Then what's your problem?" Eddie asked.

Howie stepped into the shadows and waited for his friends to gather around. "I've been watching Mrs. Jeepers," he said. "And I don't like what I see."

"That makes sense," Eddie said. "Teachers are never fun to watch. You should watch me instead."

Howie rolled his eyes. "You don't understand," he said. "I think we have a serious problem."

Liza nodded. "A vampire teacher is definitely trouble. You're not telling us anything new."

"I believe things have just gotten worse," Howie said seriously. "Much worse. I think Mrs. Jeepers is planning a space journey of her own. If I'm right, it won't be long before Mrs. Jeepers has everyone at BLAST in her control. Then it's bye-bye Bailey City and hello space shuttle."

"That's great!" Eddie yelped. "If Mrs.

Jeepers blasts into space, then she'll be out of our hair for good. We should be celebrating!"

Melody grabbed Eddie. "You're wrong," she said. "Do you know what would happen if Mrs. Jeepers became an astronaut?"

"Sure," Eddie said with a laugh. "She'd be a vampernaut!"

Melody didn't laugh at her friend's joke. "All of our astronauts would be turned into vampires," she explained, "and then they'd suck the blood of astronauts from other countries."

"I think we have something much more important to worry about," Howie added.

Melody shook her head. "My mom told me the world is building an International Space Station. Mrs. Jeepers taking control of BLAST means the end of the world working together to build a space station."

"What I'm talking about is more important than that," Howie told his friends.

"What could be more important than creating a place to live in space with other countries?" Liza asked.

Howie looked straight at Mrs. Jeepers and said in a whisper, "If Mrs. Jeepers is planning on taking over BLAST, she has to get control of the scientists."

Liza and Melody nodded. "That makes sense," Melody said. "So what?"

Howie gulped. "My dad is a scientist here."

Eddie laughed so hard he had to sit on the floor. "Your brains," he said as he tried to catch his breath, "have turned into giant black holes! One little teacher cannot take over the entire BLAST Camp, no matter how batty we think she is!"

"Eddie's right," Liza said, putting her hand on Howie's shoulder. "We're letting our imaginations zoom farther than Pluto."

"I hope you're right," Howie said. "Because the last thing I want is a vampire dad."

7

Mission Control

"Welcome to Mission Control," a tall, thin man with dark hair and glasses told them. It was the next morning and the kids were getting ready to go though a green door marked AUTHORIZED PERSONNEL ONLY.

"My name is Thomas and I'll be helping you practice today. A rocket scientist will be helping you with the real mission on Friday."

Carey held up her hand. "Aren't you a rocket scientist?"

Thomas smiled and shook his head. "I'm a college student, but one of these days I'll be a scientist."

Katy and Mrs. Jeepers stood near the front of the group. Mrs. Jeepers seemed like her regular batty self, but Katy

looked different. She wasn't smiling and she hadn't talked to anybody all morning. Dark circles underlined her eyes and Katy yawned so many times Liza lost count.

"Something's wrong with Katy," Liza said. "She looks like she didn't get a wink of sleep."

Howie nodded. "I bet Mrs. Jeepers kept her up all night. In vampire training."

Melody patted Howie on the back. "Don't worry. Thomas will protect us."

Thomas continued talking. "Today, we'll go over terms and steps that are important to your mission."

Eddie rolled his eyes. "That sounds very boring. Can't we just do our mission without practicing first?"

The tall man shook his head. "Not if you value your mission. Practice is an important safety factor for real astronauts."

Melody jabbed Eddie in the side. "Quit

being so mean," she said. "You're spoiling it for the rest of us."

Eddie sighed and didn't say another word while the man continued talking.

Katy walked up beside Thomas. She walked so slowly, it seemed like she moved in slow motion. She yawned again before speaking. "Is the Pluto Team ready to go inside Mission Control?"

All the kids cheered and Katy opened the green door. Thomas led their team inside. The kids stared as they entered a darkened room with a huge television screen and large panels of switches and buttons.

"Everyone take a chair and we'll discuss your positions," Thomas told them. Mrs. Jeepers and the team members each found a swivel chair. Eddie was the first to discover that the chairs had wheels.

"Whee!" Eddie yelled and rolled across the floor.

"Oh, no!" Liza said, knowing that Mrs.

Jeepers would get Eddie for sure. But Mrs. Jeepers didn't even glance at Eddie. She was talking quietly with Thomas and Katy.

Eddie was back in his place when Thomas, Katy, and Mrs. Jeepers looked up again. "Pluto Team, please put on your headsets and study the notebooks in front of you," Thomas said. "Listen for directions on your headsets and do not turn on your microphones yet. I'll be right back."

Mrs. Jeepers, Katy, and Thomas walked outside the green door. Eddie grinned and used the moment to pretend to be a rock singer with his microphone.

Howie tapped Eddie on the shoulder. "You better study your notebook."

Eddie groaned. "This is too much like math and science. I want to explore the universe and battle aliens with laser guns."

Liza pushed her microphone away from her mouth. "If you don't study,

you'll never get a chance to do those things. They don't let just anybody become an astronaut, you know."

" 'They don't let just anybody become an astronaut, you know,' " Eddie mocked, but he pushed away his microphone and opened up his notebook. Everyone was quiet when Mrs. Jeepers led Thomas and Katy back into the room.

"Oh, my gosh," Melody whispered. "Mrs. Jeepers has done it again."

"Done what?" Howie asked quietly.

Melody nodded toward Thomas. His face was a sickly green and he had dark circles under his eyes. "It looks like Mrs. Jeepers started training Thomas to be a vampernaut!"

Howie gulped. "Is my father next?"

Eddie leaned over to Howie. "Don't worry," he said. "Thomas said he's a college student. College students always look tired because they have to study so much."

Howie sighed and looked at Mrs. Jeepers. She was rubbing her green brooch and smiling her odd little half smile. "I hope you're right," Howie whispered. "Or BLAST Camp is in big trouble. And so is my dad!"

8

Bug Express

"This is cool," Eddie said, carefully folding the parachute to his rocket.

Melody pushed a piece of black hair off her sweaty forehead. "Actually," she said, "it's burning up in here. Don't they have air-conditioning?"

It was already Thursday and the kids weren't thinking about vampires. They were too busy building rockets. They were inside a small white trailer that was filled with tables. Each table was covered with materials to make small rockets.

"I am sorry," Katy told the kids, but she didn't sound like it. Her voice was tired and she didn't even smile. "The air-conditioning is broken. We'll open the windows to let in a breeze. We must fin- ish our rockets quickly." When Katy opened a window beside Melody's table, a giant black bug zoomed inside the room.

Eddie didn't seem to mind. Instead, he grinned and dove after the bug. Howie was too busy watching Katy to worry about bugs. "Have you noticed Katy looks even worse today?" Howie whispered to Melody.

Melody shrugged. "She looks worn-out. Most adults say keeping up with Eddie is exhausting."

Howie didn't look convinced. Instead of working on his rocket, he watched Mrs. Jeepers talking to Katy in the far corner of the huge room. Thomas came in to help Katy, but he ended up staring out the window as if he were in a daze.

Finally the kids were almost finished. Eddie held up his rocket. It was blue and white with a red nose cone and about as long as his arm. He had painted the words BUG EXPRESS on the side of his rocket. "I'm already finished with mine,"

Eddie bragged. "Let's go launch these babies."

"That looks great," Liza said, admiring Eddie's rocket. "But are you sure you followed all the steps?"

"Of course," Eddie snapped. "I can follow directions."

"Why did you name it *Bug Express*?" Melody asked.

Eddie grinned and pointed to the clear, hollow section of his rocket. "Because of Herman here," Eddie explained.

"Herman?" Howie asked.

Eddie nodded. "Herman the bug. He'll be a bugstronaut."

Liza stared at the beetle inside Eddie's rocket. "That's horrible," she said. "Poor little bug, how could you send him up in a rocket like that?"

"Don't forget," Howie reminded her. "the U.S. Space Program sent monkeys up in space before men. They made it back to Earth just fine."

"Well, if the space program is looking for monkeys, then Eddie better watch out," Melody joked.

"Very funny, banana brains," Eddie said. Then he zoomed his rocket around the room. Liza stopped him to make sure Herman was okay. She even insisted Eddie open the rocket every few minutes to make sure the bug had enough air.

"Why don't you stop racing around and help me paint my rocket?" Liza finally asked Eddie.

"I'm too busy," Eddie told her. "You'll have to do it yourself."

"I'll help you," Melody said. Howie pitched in, too. When they were finished with Liza's rocket, the three kids worked together to finish Melody's and Howie's rockets, too. Finally all the kids were done designing their rockets.

Mrs. Jeepers rubbed her brooch and looked at Katy. "It is time to fly," Mrs. Jeepers said.

Katy stared at Mrs. Jeepers' brooch

and nodded. "It is time to fly the rockets," Katy repeated slowly. "Please follow me."

All the kids cheered and headed out the door with Mrs. Jeepers and Katy leading the way. Thomas stayed behind and stared out the window. The Pluto Team, Mrs. Jeepers, and Katy walked down a long gravel road to a big field. Katy gave each kid an engine that they had to carefully stick in the bottom of their rockets.

Eddie was the first kid to put his rocket on the launchpad. He pushed a red button that was attached to the pad. The button ignited the rocket engine and BAM! Eddie's *Bug Express* blasted into the sky. Slowly, the parachute started to open, but then it got stuck. It only opened part of the way and the rocket dropped back to Earth and landed with a hard thump.

"I hope Herman's okay," Liza said quietly.

One by one, every kid blasted his or her rocket off. Huey's rocket landed in a

tree. Jake's rocket almost went onto the gravel road, and Carey's parachute got stuck on a power line before the wind blew it to the ground.

Eddie hurried to snatch his rocket from a clump of weeds. When he opened the clear, hollow section, Herman spread his wings and zoomed quickly out of Eddie's reach. "He can tell the other bugs how cool it was to blast off," Eddie laughed.

"I'm glad your parachute opened part of the way," Melody told Eddie, "or your bug would be splattered all over the ground."

Mrs. Jeepers stood behind the third-graders, staring at each rocket as it blasted off. "Herman is a lucky bug," their teacher said. "Flying is so exciting. It would be wonderful to explore beyond the clouds. Who knows?" she added with her little half smile. "Someday maybe I will get a chance."

"Collect your rockets," Katy told the kids in her tired voice. "It is time to go."

As the kids walked back to the BLAST Center, Howie lagged behind. "What's wrong?" Melody asked Howie.

"Didn't you hear Mrs. Jeepers? It's only a matter of time before she takes over BLAST Camp," Howie told her, "and then we'll all be bug splat."

9

Lunch with Vampires

The kids went through the BLAST Camp lunch line, picking up pizza, cookies, apples, and milk. "This looks tasty," Eddie said, taking a bite of his pizza before he even sat down.

"How can you think of food at a time like this?" Howie asked. Howie sat at the far end of a long table. His friends sat around him. Eddie was the only one eating.

Eddie spoke with his mouth full. "I'm hungry," he mumbled, shrugging his shoulders. In just a few minutes Eddie had finished his food and was drawing a creature on his pizza-stained paper napkin. The creature had three heads, five arms, and only one foot.

Mrs. Jeepers walked behind Eddie with

her tray. It was empty, except for two bottles of tomato juice. Mrs. Jeepers stopped suddenly and stared at Eddie's drawing. "What have you drawn?" she asked Eddie.

Eddie quickly made up a name. "It's an alien from the planet Thurrow."

Mrs. Jeepers picked up the napkin and examined it closely. "What a very interesting creature. I would like to meet him someday."

Eddie grinned. "I hope you do," he said firmly as Mrs. Jeepers walked over to sit with Katy.

"Did you hear that?" Melody asked. "Mrs. Jeepers can't wait to round up a bunch of aliens and have them take over BLAST Camp. We have to do something."

"It's worse than we thought," Liza said slowly. She nodded toward Mrs. Jeepers' table. Katy, Thomas, and five scientists in lab coats sat around Mrs. Jeepers. Every one of them had two bottles of tomato juice in front of them.

"If this keeps up, Mrs. Jeepers will have

every scientist slurping vampire cocktails by the end of the week," Melody said.

The kids gasped when Howie's dad waved at them and then went to join Mrs. Jeepers' table.

"At least your dad has a tray of food," Eddie said.

Melody patted Howie on the back. "Mrs. Jeepers doesn't have him in her clutches yet."

Howie covered his throat with his hands. "Having a vampire teacher is bad enough, but I don't want a vampire sleeping in the same house as me! We have to keep her from taking over the camp before it's too late."

Liza opened her milk carton and asked, "How can we do that?"

Melody smiled. "I have the perfect way to stop Mrs. Jeepers," she said. "We'll start right after lunch, but I'll need your help."

Eddie shook his head. "I didn't come to BLAST Camp to battle vampires-in-training. Count me out of your plan."

"I'm ready to help," Liza said. "After all, Howie is our friend."

"Tell us your plan," Howie said to Melody.

But Melody didn't have a chance to explain because Katy walked up to them.

"Let's hurry," Katy told the trainees, "so we have time to browse in the museum before we try out our next piece of equipment."

The rest of the kids gobbled their food and hurried to line up behind Katy as she led them to the museum. Melody took a few bites before joining the rest of the Pluto Team.

Katy remained at the entrance of the museum while Mrs. Jeepers and the kids wandered around. Mrs. Jeepers stood in front of a full-size model of the *Apollo VII* space capsule.

Melody walked up to her teacher and pointed to the model. "I've heard that Mission Control ran out of the drink you had at lunch. They won't have it again at

BLAST Camp," Melody told Mrs. Jeepers.

Mrs. Jeepers smiled her odd little half smile. "I do not worry about that," Mrs. Jeepers said before walking off to study a Space Lab replica.

Liza tapped Melody on the shoulder. "Why did you lie to Mrs. Jeepers?" Liza asked.

"That's my plan," Melody explained. "We

have to make BLAST Camp sound so bad that Mrs. Jeepers won't want to take it over."

"Lying isn't right," Liza insisted.

"I know," Melody admitted, "but we have to do something."

"Let me try," Howie said. He hurried up the steps to the Space Lab model. "Mrs. Jeepers," Howie said, "did you know that staying too long at BLAST Camp makes you forget everything you know?"

Mrs. Jeepers looked at Howie and rubbed her green brooch. "I believe you are incorrect about that," she said before walking away.

"Your plan isn't working very well," Howie told Melody.

"Maybe we can tell her there are no coffins in space," Melody suggested.

Eddie shook his head. "Space is perfect for vampires. It's dark and it would be easy for them to fly since there's no gravity."

Liza frowned at Eddie. "You're not helping matters any. We have to think of ways to make BLAST Camp and space sound bad — not good."

The kids tried to think of something else to say to Mrs. Jeepers while they were waiting in line to use the MMU. "This is the Manned Mobile Unit," Katy explained. "It allowed astronauts more freedom in space, but it is no longer used because it was too dangerous. Does anyone know why?"

Howie raised his hand. "Since it wasn't

attached to anything, someone could get lost in space."

Katy patted the big white piece of machinery. "That's exactly right," she said. "Now we use other equipment to maneuver in space. We'll try that later. Now, who wants to be first to try the MMU?"

Melody stopped Eddie from raising his hand. "We have to talk to Mrs. Jeepers," she said.

"You guys take all the fun out of everything," Eddie complained, but he followed his friends over to Mrs. Jeepers.

"Guess what?" Howie said to Mrs. Jeepers. "I heard that BLAST Camp is going to have a whole group of cheerleaders here next week. Just think how noisy they'll be."

Mrs. Jeepers frowned at Howie, but continued watching Jake turn himself sideways on the MMU. The machinery looked like a huge chair. When Jake squeezed the control he flipped over to his other side.

"Ooh," Liza moaned, holding her stomach. "That makes my stomach feel weird."

"It doesn't look as scary as the Multi-Axis Trainer," Howie said.

"Liza," Katy called across the room. "It's your turn." Liza snapped on the helmet and climbed onto the tall machine. After turning sideways and swirling around, Liza looked green.

"What's wrong with you?" Melody asked Liza when she got off.

"I ate my pizza too fast," Liza said. "I think I'm sick."

Howie rubbed his stomach. "I don't feel very well, either," he said.

"You guys are wimps," Eddie said.

"That's me," Liza said, sitting down and putting her head between her knees.

Melody sat down on the floor beside Liza and watched Mrs. Jeepers maneuver the MMU perfectly. "We'd better come up with another plan," Melody said. "It looks like Mrs. Jeepers has learned everything and is ready to take over the camp!"

10

Space Spies

Eddie held his stomach, rolled his eyes, and groaned. "Now I'm feeling sick, too," he said.

"The MMU finally got to you," Melody said with a nod.

"No," Eddie said with a shake of his head. "YOU finally got to me, and you're making me sicker than eating green cheese!"

"Eddie's right," Liza said. "We've been here for four days, and so far all Mrs. Jeepers has done is study star charts and learn to use the machines. That doesn't mean anything. After all, she's a teacher. Teachers spend their lives studying and reading."

"Finally," Eddie said. "Somebody besides me has developed a brain."

"I've had brains all along," Howie said. "That's why I've been thinking."

"Well, stop that," Eddie argued. "Thinking gets us into messes every time!"

"But what if Mrs. Jeepers really is planning to take over BLAST Camp?" Melody asked Eddie. "She'll be able to train an entire troop of vampernauts. This could be the end of life as we know it."

Eddie clapped his hands over his ears. "If you don't stop talking about space vampires, I agree this will be the end of one thing — our friendship!"

Liza gasped. "You don't mean it, do you?"

Eddie nodded. "I've been listening to this stuff all week when I could have been having fun. And that's the one thing friends are good for . . . having fun!"

"Friends stick together," Howie pointed out. "Even when it's not fun."

"I'd have to be Krazy Glue to stick to you," Eddie said with a laugh, "because

you're all lunatics — or should I say lunar-tics!"

"This is no laughing matter," Melody said. "We could be in serious trouble."

"That's right," Liza agreed. "All the scientists at lunch already look like they're soldiers in Mrs. Jeepers' vampire mission. Howie's dad could be next!"

"You're going to have to come up with more proof than star maps and sleepy trainers to convince me," Eddie told them.

"Then we'll do what all good detectives do," Howie said.

"What?" Liza and Melody asked together.

"We'll find evidence that our teacher is a space vampire," Howie told them. "And we'll do it tonight!"

That night, all four kids put on pajamas over their regular clothes. They hid flashlights under their pillows. Then they lay still, waiting for everyone else to fall asleep. When everything in the Female Habitat had been silent for an hour, Melody slipped out of her bunk. She tapped Liza on the shoulder and together the girls crept along the concrete floor and out the door. Eddie and Howie were waiting for them near the Waste Elimination door.

Eddie yawned. "I can't believe I'm losing good sleep just to sneak around a space playground," he complained.

"We're not sneaking around," Howie pointed out.

Melody nodded. "We're spies," she added. "Space spies."

Eddie grinned. "When it comes to spying, I'm an expert," he said. "Follow me!"

Eddie led the way. Howie followed. Liza and Melody came next. The four kids sneaked along the silent corridors, their tiny flashlights barely cutting through the black night. Eddie stopped in front of a door labeled SENIOR TRAINEE JEEPERS.

"What are you doing?" Liza hissed to Eddie.

"I'll prove Mrs. Jeepers is just a regular teacher when you see her sleeping like a newborn kitten," Eddie told his friends.

"We shouldn't go in there," Liza said with a whimper. "Vampires don't sleep at night. She may be waiting to swoop down on us and suck our blood!"

"She'll only come after you if she likes the taste of chicken," Eddie said, "because that's what you are!"

Before anybody could argue, Eddie grabbed the handle and pulled. The door silently swung open and Eddie slipped into Mrs. Jeepers' sleeping quarters. Howie, Melody, and Liza looked over Eddie's shoulder as he slowly panned his flashlight around the room. There, in the corner, was Mrs. Jeepers' bunk.

Liza groaned. Melody gasped. Mrs. Jeepers' bunk was empty, and the covers weren't even wrinkled. "It looks like Mrs.

Jeepers hasn't been in this bed all week," Melody said.

"Of course not," Liza said with a shaky voice. "Vampires never sleep at night."

Howie put his hand on Eddie's shoulder. "Your plan has backfired," Howie said. "You just proved our teacher is definitely a vampire."

"Don't be ridiculous," Eddie said, but he didn't sound very sure. "All we have to do is find Mrs. Jeepers and you'll get a good explanation for this."

"You don't mean you're planning to go on a vampire hunt, do you?" Melody asked.

"That," Eddie said, "is exactly what I mean."

Eddie hurried out of Mrs. Jeepers' room and down the hall. His friends rushed after him. "She has to be somewhere," Eddie said as he poked his head in every door he passed. "Teachers never disappear."

"I don't like this," Liza said, looking over her shoulder into the dark hallway.

"What if we find Mrs. Jeepers?" Melody asked with a squeaky voice.

"What if we find her and she's not alone?" Howie gulped.

Liza grabbed Melody's arm. "What if she's having a vampire conference?" Liza asked.

Melody shook her head. "Vampires haven't taken over BLAST Camp yet. We're going to stop her before that happens."

"Unless someone stops us first," Howie said. "I think I hear something."

The kids stopped in the middle of the dark hallway and listened. *Beep. Beep. Squeak. Click.*

"Is that an alien?" Liza whispered.

"Sounds more like a refrigerator to me," Eddie said.

"Let's go back to our rooms before it's too late," Liza begged.

"Don't worry," Melody said. "We're all in this together."

"Let's keep going," Eddie said, starting off down the dark hallway.

They were getting close to Mission Control Center when Melody grabbed Eddie. His sneakers squeaked to a stop. "Shhh," Melody said. "There's the sound again."

The kids stood, silent as moon rocks, and listened. Beeps and crackles echoed down the corridor. "I think it's coming from there," Liza said, pointing through a window to Mission Control.

Eddie nodded. "There's only one way to find out," he said as he reached for the door and opened it just a crack.

Inside Mission Control was their teacher. Mrs. Jeepers sat at a huge console. Her hands blurred as she punched buttons, twirled knobs, and flipped switches. Colored lights blinked, casting eerie shadows over their teacher. She no

longer wore her odd little half smile. Instead, Mrs. Jeepers grinned so wide the kids could see the flashing lights glisten on her pointy eyeteeth.

Suddenly, a speaker crackled and a strange voice boomed throughout the Center. "Come in, BLAST Camp," the woman's voice said in a strange accent.

Mrs. Jeepers flipped a switch and spoke into a microphone. "I read you," their teacher said, "loud and clear."

"What is your situation?" the voice asked.

Mrs. Jeepers smiled even more. "I have mastered this technology," she said to the strange voice. "I am in control!"

"Very good," the stranger said. "Let the countdown begin!"

"What's she talking about?" Liza whispered. "This is just a camp. She can't really blast off. Can she?"

11

Mission Out of Control

Melody's eyes were wide. "Mrs. Jeepers must already have vampires in space," she said softly.

Eddie shook his head. "There's no such thing as a vampire in space, at least not yet."

It was the next morning. The four kids stared at their pancakes. None of them felt like eating.

"What if Mrs. Jeepers has a direct link to aliens?" Liza moaned.

"Maybe it was all a dream," Melody said.

"You mean a nightmare," Liza added.

"It was no dream," Howie said.

Just then, Mrs. Jeepers strode into the cafeteria, and she wasn't alone. A woman so tall she had to duck through the door walked beside their teacher. The stranger had jet-black hair that came down to a point on her forehead, and her eyes were the same green as Mrs. Jeepers' brooch. Mrs. Jeepers and the stranger sat at a nearby table, both of them sipping tomato juice.

Howie gulped when he heard them. "Mrs. Jeepers wasn't talking to an alien or a space vampire last night. Listen."

Sure enough, the voice they heard was identical to the one on the speaker the night before. Suddenly, the stranger laughed. When she did, the kids couldn't help noticing the stranger's two pointy eyeteeth.

"Who says she isn't a space vampire?" Eddie asked. "She looks pretty weird to me."

Liza's face turned as pale as the milk in her glass. "Howie was right," she whispered. "Mrs. Jeepers and her batty friends *are* invading BLAST Camp! Then they're going to take over everything!"

"We have to do something," Howie said. "We only have one day left to save BLAST Camp."

"All our other plans failed," Melody said and put her head down on the table. "We're doomed."

Even Eddie looked scared. "Don't worry," he said. "I've never let a teacher get the best of me yet."

"Do you have an idea?" Liza asked hopefully.

Eddie didn't have a chance to answer because just then Katy entered the room. She looked like she was sleepwalking. Dark circles outlined her eyes, and when she spoke her voice sounded as flat as the pancakes on the kids' plates. "It is time," Katy said. "Please come with me."

Mrs. Jeepers and the stranger hurried to catch up with Katy. The rest of the trainees followed as Katy led them outside Mission Control.

"We have a special guest today," Katy said once they were there, pointing to

Mrs. Jeepers' friend. "Dr. Vametta will help you finish preparing for your first shuttle mission."

"This is even worse than I imagined," Howie whispered. "Dr. Vametta is here to help Mrs. Jeepers take over BLAST Camp."

Dr. Vametta stepped up beside Katy and nodded at all the trainees. "This is what you and Thomas trained for earlier in the week," Dr. Vametta said. "It is time to test your knowledge. Your team's challenge is to repair a communications satellite. Each of you will be assigned a crew position."

Katy moved throughout the group of trainees and told them their jobs. Liza and Howie nodded as they received their positions as mission specialists. Melody was assigned to be a mission scientist.

"Give me something good," Eddie said when Katy stood in front of him.

Katy smiled. "You," she said, "will be the commander. The responsibility of a successful mission for the Pluto Team rests upon your shoulders." And then Katy walked on, leaving Liza, Melody, and Howie staring at Eddie.

"Oh, no," Liza finally groaned. "With Eddie as our commander, we'll be a mission out of control!"

"Hey." Eddie grinned. "Just remember, I'm in charge!"

Howie shook his head. "A good commander isn't bossy. He knows the entire crew has to work together," he warned.

Eddie rubbed his hands together and grinned. "Forget the lecture," he told his friends. "This is only a space game, so get ready to blast off with me as your leader!"

"We don't have time to play games," Liza reminded Eddie. "We have another job to do."

Melody nodded. "And we're running out of time. Look!"

Mrs. Jeepers walked right up to the kids. "Let us take our places in the flight simulator," she told the four of them.

"You mean," Melody said with a gulp, "you're going with us?"

"But of course," Mrs. Jeepers said. "I am your pilot!"

Melody grabbed her friends when Mrs. Jeepers disappeared into the nearby flight simulator. On the outside, the simulator looked like a small space shuttle. "We're about to be trapped by a vampire teacher and her batty friend," she said, pointing to Dr. Vametta.

Dr. Vametta sat at the Mission Control panel. The kids could see her through a small window. Dr. Vametta looked serious. Dead serious.

"What are we going to do?" Liza asked.

"Whatever it is," Howie said, "we'll have to do it from in there!"

Katy motioned for the kids to take their places in the flight simulator. Silently, they found their seats and buckled up. "This is neat," Eddie said, looking at all the buttons. "It's like a real shuttle."

"Look out the window." Liza pointed to

the monitor designed to look like a window. "It's just like what you'd see from the real shuttle."

The countdown began, and soon the kids felt the roar of the blastoff. Out the window they saw the ground below. They remembered everything they had learned as their craft soared into space. Dr. Vametta, Carey, Jake, and Huey gave directions and support from the command center.

"This is very exciting," Liza said under her breath.

Melody stared in amazement as the window showed Earth getting farther and farther away. "This is exactly how the astronauts must feel," Melody whispered.

Mrs. Jeepers turned to look at Liza and Melody and smiled so wide they saw her pointy eyeteeth. "Who knows, maybe someday we will be real astronauts," Mrs. Jeepers said.

Liza gulped and looked at Melody.

Melody patted Liza on the shoulder and flipped a switch. Liza flipped the switches she was responsible for and began punching a series of buttons. Soon all the kids forgot about vampires and aliens as they worked to complete their mission, fixing a broken communication satellite. They worked so hard, they forgot it wasn't a real mission. It seemed real to them.

"This is very important," Howie said. "The whole world depends on these satellites."

Liza carefully dressed in a space suit and left the ship through the air lock. As a mission specialist, it was her job to go into space to repair the satellite. Mrs. Jeepers concentrated on checking their course. Melody used the robot arm to grasp the satellite and bring it in closer for Liza to work on. Liza started fixing the satellite according to the directions Howie gave her. Howie watched Liza and the satellite through a rear window.

But Eddie didn't help. He didn't seem interested in working with anyone. He was having too much fun all by himself, flipping switches and saying, "Roger, Mission Control," into his headset microphone.

"Eddie," Howie said, "you need to slow down. You're way ahead of schedule."

"Don't worry about me," Eddie snapped. "You just take care of yourself."

Howie shook his head. "We're supposed to work together. Remember? We're the Pluto Team."

Eddie was having too much fun to pay attention. He reached across Howie and mashed several buttons all at once.

Suddenly, their capsule jerked away from the satellite. It pitched, it rolled, it yawed.

"Watch out!" Melody screamed. "We're going to crash!"

12

Vampire Milk Shake

Liza stomped up to Eddie in her space suit. It was after their mission and the team was standing outside the shuttle. Liza pulled off her helmet and pointed a gloved finger at him. "How could you?" she asked. "You left me in outer space. I was a goner!"

"We all would have died if Mrs. Jeepers hadn't pulled us out of our spin at the last minute," Howie said.

"You've ruined our mission," Melody told Eddie.

"You've ruined everything all week," Liza said.

"Thanks to you, Pluto Team failed," Howie added.

Eddie shrugged. "I didn't mean to spoil the mission. I was just trying to have fun."

"Haven't you learned anything? Sometimes you have to work before having fun," Liza said.

"You're starting to sound as batty as Mrs. Jeepers," Eddie complained.

Howie grabbed Eddie's arm. "That's it!" he said. "You just solved our vampernaut problem."

Liza and Melody looked at Howie. "What are you talking about?" Melody asked.

"I think I figured out a way to save my dad from becoming a vampire-in-training," Howie said with a grin. "All we have to do is convince Mrs. Jeepers that she must leave BLAST Camp."

"How do you plan to do that?" Melody asked.

"It's easy," Howie said. "We'll use Eddie!"

"Don't count me in on your airheaded plan," Eddie said.

Liza poked Eddie in the chest. "After messing up our entire mission, the least

you can do is listen to Howie's plan.
After all, you are our friend."

Melody nodded. "And friends stick together . . . even when it isn't fun."

Eddie looked at his friends. "All right,"
he finally said. "What do I have to do?"

"Just be yourself!" Howie said with a
grin. Then he pulled his friends close and
told them his plan.

"Wait a minute," Eddie said when

Howie finished. "I never agreed to be vampire bait."

"I don't blame Eddie for being scared," Melody said. "Your plan could backfire. Then we'd all end up as a vampire's milk shake."

"We have to be brave," Howie said. "It's up to us to save BLAST Camp. And my dad."

"Howie's right," Melody said.

Liza nodded. Then they all looked at Eddie. "The success of Howie's secret mission depends on you," Melody told Eddie. "Are you part of our team?"

Eddie took a deep breath. "You can count on me," he said.

He had barely finished talking before Mrs. Jeepers and Katy appeared. "It's now or never," Howie whispered to Eddie. "Are you ready?"

"Roger," Eddie said. "Secret-weapon Eddie is ready to launch on your command."

13

Secret-Weapon Eddie

Katy and Mrs. Jeepers came up behind Liza, Melody, Howie, and Eddie. "I am happy that you are finally working together," Mrs. Jeepers said.

"Our training missions are serious," Katy added. "Real astronauts train so they'll know what to do in case of an emergency. Mrs. Jeepers is a hero for her quick thinking in saving the mission."

Dr. Vametta came up and put her bony hand on Mrs. Jeepers' shoulder. "Thank goodness your teacher can think under pressure. That is what an astronaut must be able to do. And, of course, work well with team members." Dr. Vametta frowned at Eddie.

Eddie jumped at his chance. "Work,

work, work," he said. "Is that all teachers can think about? You should think about fun for a change."

Mrs. Jeepers flashed her eyes at Eddie, but Liza spoke up before Mrs. Jeepers had a chance to say a word. "Work *can* be fun," Liza said sweetly.

"Mrs. Jeepers taught us that," Melody added in her most polite voice.

Howie nodded. "Haven't you learned anything this year?" he asked Eddie.

"Learning is for school, and this isn't school!" To prove his point, Eddie zoomed across the room like a shooting star and headed straight for the robot arm. He grabbed the controls and tried to pinch Carey's pigtail. Of course, the arm swung madly out of control and bopped Jake on the nose.

"Stop!" Thomas hollered. "You're messing up the robot!"

Mrs. Jeepers took a step in Eddie's direction, but Liza stepped in front of her.

"Eddie needs to learn more about simple machines before he can operate a robot, don't you think?"

Mrs. Jeepers looked down at Liza and nodded. "Science is important for all third-graders to learn."

Eddie shot like a meteor over to the Mission Control panel of buttons and switches. A group of kids from the Venus Team was trying to figure out how much fuel they would need to complete their mission. They were adding up a long line of numbers.

Eddie looked over their shoulders. "Three plus three is sixty-four," he told them. "Add that to five plus seven plus eleven and you should get eighteen bazillion and three. Subtract that from two times eight plus ten minus the distance from the sun to the moon and your answer is forty-two!"

"Poor Eddie," Melody said to Mrs. Jeepers before she could walk over to him. "He just doesn't do very well in math. He needs more practice before he can be a pilot."

Mrs. Jeepers nodded. "Perhaps you are right," she said slowly.

Katy headed for Eddie. "Stop," she warned him, "before you ruin the Venus Team's work!"

Eddie slipped away from Katy's grasp, dodged Dr. Vametta, and raced around Thomas. He didn't stop until he reached

the Manned Mobile Unit. "Watch this!" Eddie yelled.

Eddie strapped himself into the MMU and gripped the controls. Thomas scrambled out of the way as Eddie flew between Dr. Vametta and Katy. Three more scientists dove for cover. "Wheeee!" Eddie yelled.

"Quick!" Howie hollered. "Head left before you crash into the space shuttle!"

Eddie pulled on the controls, but instead of flying safely left he turned right and headed straight for Mrs. Jeepers.

"NO!" Howie yelled at Eddie. "That's the wrong way!"

"Watch out!" Thomas yelled.

Eddie jerked on the controls. The MMU pitched. It rolled. It yawed. Suddenly, Eddie veered away from Mrs. Jeepers. Thomas and Katy worked together to grab the MMU and got it under control before Eddie crashed into the Uranus Team.

Mrs. Jeepers' hand reached for her brooch. Liza crossed her fingers. Melody closed her eyes. But Howie stood right in front of Mrs. Jeepers and shook his head. "Poor Eddie. He never understood the directions. I guess he hasn't learned as much as the rest of us," he told Mrs. Jeepers.

Melody opened her eyes and nodded. "He needs more practice."

"And more homework," Liza added.

Mrs. Jeepers' hand was only an inch away from the green stone in her brooch when Dr. Vametta glided over to Mrs. Jeepers.

"Shall we attempt our mission again?" Dr. Vametta asked.

Mrs. Jeepers looked at Dr. Vametta. She looked at the space shuttle. Then she looked at Eddie and smiled her odd little half smile. "There is no need to try again. I will call for our bus. We must head back to Bailey School. I have an important mission awaiting me there!"

That afternoon, the kids waited in front of BLAST Camp. Mrs. Jeepers stood at the front of the line as the Bailey School bus pulled to a stop.

"Where's Katy?" Liza asked. "Isn't she going to say good-bye?"

Her question was answered when the door to BLAST Camp swished open and Howie's dad walked out and made an announcement to all the students from Bailey Elementary.

"Sorry, kids," Howie's dad said with a

smile. "Katy and the other trainers are worn-out. They sent me out here to tell you good-bye."

Liza, Melody, Howie, and Eddie looked at one another and smiled.

Melody slapped Howie on the back. "Mission accomplished," she said.

"Your plan worked," Liza said. "Eddie convinced Mrs. Jeepers that she's needed at Bailey Elementary School."

Eddie kicked at a clump of rocks. "I don't think Howie's plan worked right," he said seriously.

"Why not?" Melody, Howie, and Liza asked together.

"Because Mrs. Jeepers is probably planning to dump three tons of homework on me," Eddie complained. "I'll have to come up with another plan to get out of doing extra work!"

"Oh, no," Liza said with a laugh. "BLAST Camp is safe from Mrs. Jeepers, but Bailey School will never be safe from Eddie!"

Authors' Note

BLAST Camp is a made-up place in Bailey City. Readers should be aware that there are real space camps run by NASA. There are three locations: Alabama, Florida, and California.

Debbie Dadey and Marcia Thornton Jones have fun writing stories together. When they both worked at an elementary school in Lexington, Kentucky, Debbie was the school librarian and Marcia was a teacher. During their lunch break in the school cafeteria, they came up with the idea of the Bailey School kids.

Recently Debbie and her family moved to Aurora, Illinois. Marcia and her husband still live in Kentucky, where she continues to teach. How do these authors still write together? They talk on the phone and use computers and fax machines!

Out-of-This-World Activities

Moon-Dust Cookies

You will need a grown-up to help you with this recipe.

1½ cups flour
¼ teaspoon salt
¼ teaspoon baking powder
1 cup butter
1¾ cups sugar
2 eggs
1 teaspoon vanilla extract
1 cup chocolate chips
½ cup chopped nuts (walnuts or other)
3 teaspoons ground cinnamon
2 teaspoons cocoa powder

In a small bowl, mix together the flour, baking powder, and salt. In a large bowl, beat the butter and 1½ cups of the sugar until smooth. Beat in the eggs one at a time, followed by the vanilla. Add the flour mixture and mix well. Stir in the chocolate chips and nuts. Then put the dough in the refrigerator to make it easier to handle. In a small, shallow bowl, combine the rest of the sugar with the cinnamon and cocoa powder. After about 15 minutes, take the dough out of the refrigerator and shape it into 1-inch balls. Roll each ball in the cinnamon-cocoa sugar and then place them 2 inches apart on an ungreased cookie sheet. Bake at 400° F for 8–10 minutes, or until pale brown. Makes about 5–6 dozen totally spacey cookies!

Rocket Fuel

You will need a grown-up to help you with this recipe.

1 sliced banana
1 cup sliced strawberries
½ cup apple juice or orange juice
½ cup vanilla frozen yogurt

Put all the ingredients in a blender and combine until smooth. Pour some for you and a friend, and prepare to blast off!

A Spacey Maze

You are a Mission Control Specialist. Can you help this astronaut get back to his shuttle?

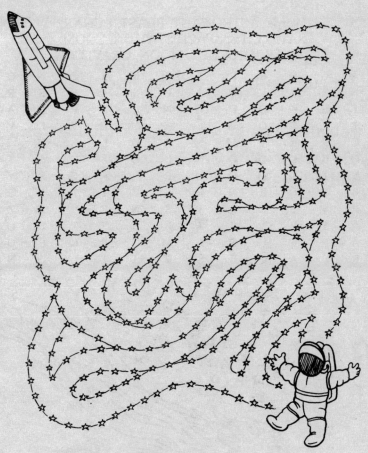

Answer on page 124

A Galaxy Word Search

Find the words hidden in the galaxy below. Words can be horizontal, vertical, diagonal, and even backward!

Words: ASTRONAUT, BLAST, LUNAR, SATELLITE, SPACE STATION, ZOOM, MARS, ROCKET, MOON, GRAVITY

```
A  G  D  E  R  Z  J  K  S  Q  N  G
N  Z  R  V  U  A  O  M  A  R  S  R
T  E  O  O  I  G  N  L  T  P  R  A
T  A  C  O  W  I  X  U  E  V  L  V
C  R  K  T  M  M  A  O  L  N  H  I
O  K  E  Q  O  N  L  O  L  F  S  T
V  J  T  D  O  H  P  N  I  G  R  Y
B  Y  Q  R  N  R  G  P  T  T  Y  S
R  M  T  U  K  V  S  N  E  W  A  Z
N  S  P  T  S  A  L  B  S  T  L  O
A  R  F  U  S  L  M  G  P  K  S  O
S  P  A  C  E  S  T  A  T  I  O  N
```

Answer on page 124

Out-of-This-World Planet Game

Here's a sentence to help you remember the names of all the planets in the solar system in order. The first letter of each word begins the name of each planet.

My Very Excellent Mother Just Sent Us Nine Pizzas.

Or make up your own sentence with your friends. Set it to music and make your own out-of-this-world song!

Mercury
Venus
Earth
Mars
Jupiter
Saturn
Uranus
Neptune
Pluto

A Crossword Puzzle Blast

Now that you've read *Mrs. Jeepers in Outer Space,* do you know the answers to this puzzle?

Across
1. What is the last name of the special guest Mrs. Jeepers brings to BLAST camp?
2. What color is the nose cone of Eddie's rocket?
3. What is the name of the bug Eddie launched in his rocket?
4. The Pluto Team's mission was to fix a broken _____.

Down
1. What do you call a vampire in outer space?
5. What is the fourth planet from the sun?
6. _____'s dad arranges for the third-graders to go to space camp.

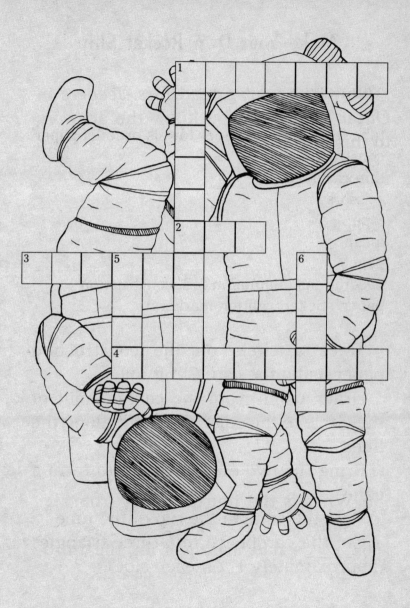

Answer on page 124

Make Your Own Rocket Ship

You need:

tube from a roll of paper towels or toilet paper
construction paper
thin cardboard
scissors
tape
a can
pencil
decorations (aluminum foil, construction
paper, stickers, glitter, markers)

Trace a circle on the construction paper using the can. Cut it out.

Draw a line from the center point of the circle to the edge. Cut a slit along the line.

Bring the two ends together to form a cone.

Tape the cone to the top of the tube.

Cut the cardboard into three triangles (approximately 1" on each side).

Cut three slits in the bottom of the tube (approximately 1" high).

Slide one triangle into each slit with the point facing up.

Decorate your rocket with aluminum foil, stickers, construction paper, glitter, and/or markers.

Countdown till blastoff!

Fun Planet Facts!

- Mercury is the hottest planet by day, but it is super-cold at night.
- Mars has the biggest volcano in the solar system — Olympus Mons.
- Rusted iron in the rocks on Mars makes the planet look red.
- Jupiter, Saturn, Uranus, and Neptune are not solid like Earth. They're mostly made of hot, swirling gases. (Spaceships can't land on them. It would be like landing on a cloud.)
- Ganymede is the biggest moon in the solar system. It belongs to Jupiter and is even bigger than the planet Mercury.
- Saturn has more moons than any other planet in the solar system — 18.
- Uranus is tilted like a top spinning on its side.
- Neptune's Great Dark Spot is a storm that is always brewing and is the size of a planet itself.

- Sometimes Pluto's orbit crisscrosses Neptune's, bringing it closer to the sun.

Puzzle Answers

A Spacey Maze

A Crossword Puzzle Blast

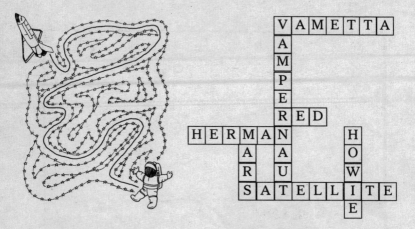

Galaxy Word Search

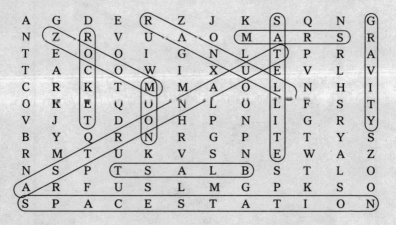